Quentin Blake

THE GREEN SHIP

RED FOX

For Joan Aiken

A Red Fox Book

Published by Random House Children's Publishers UK
61-63 Uxbridge Road, London W5 5 SA

A Division of The Random House Group Ltd
Addresses for companies within The Random House Group Limited can be found
at: www.randomhouse.co.uk/offices.htm

23

First published in Great Britain by
Jonathan Cape 1998
Red Fox edition 2000

Printed in China

The Random House Group Limited Reg. No. 954009

www.randomhousechildrens.co.uk

ISBN 978 0 099 25332 7

I can remember very clearly, even now, what it was like when we climbed over the wall into the garden of the big house. We knew we weren't supposed to, but we had been staying with our aunt for a fortnight already, and were beginning to feel bored — so we were on the lookout for an adventure.

Over the wall it wasn't much like the kind of garden we were used to; more like a park, or even a forest.
"We can be explorers," Alice said, crashing into the undergrowth. "I wonder what we shall discover?"
The trees were huge and covered with ivy; it really was very like a jungle.

We plunged deeper and deeper into it. We thought we were completely lost; then all at once we pushed aside a screen of branches and saw something absolutely astonishing.

It was a ship. At least, it wasn't a real ship; but you could see it was meant to be a ship. Bushes had been cut into the shape of the bows and stern, and two trees trimmed to look like funnels. On either side of these there were two tall thin trees with not many branches that were obviously meant to be the masts.

Then Alice said: "Come on. There's nobody about. Let's get a look at it."

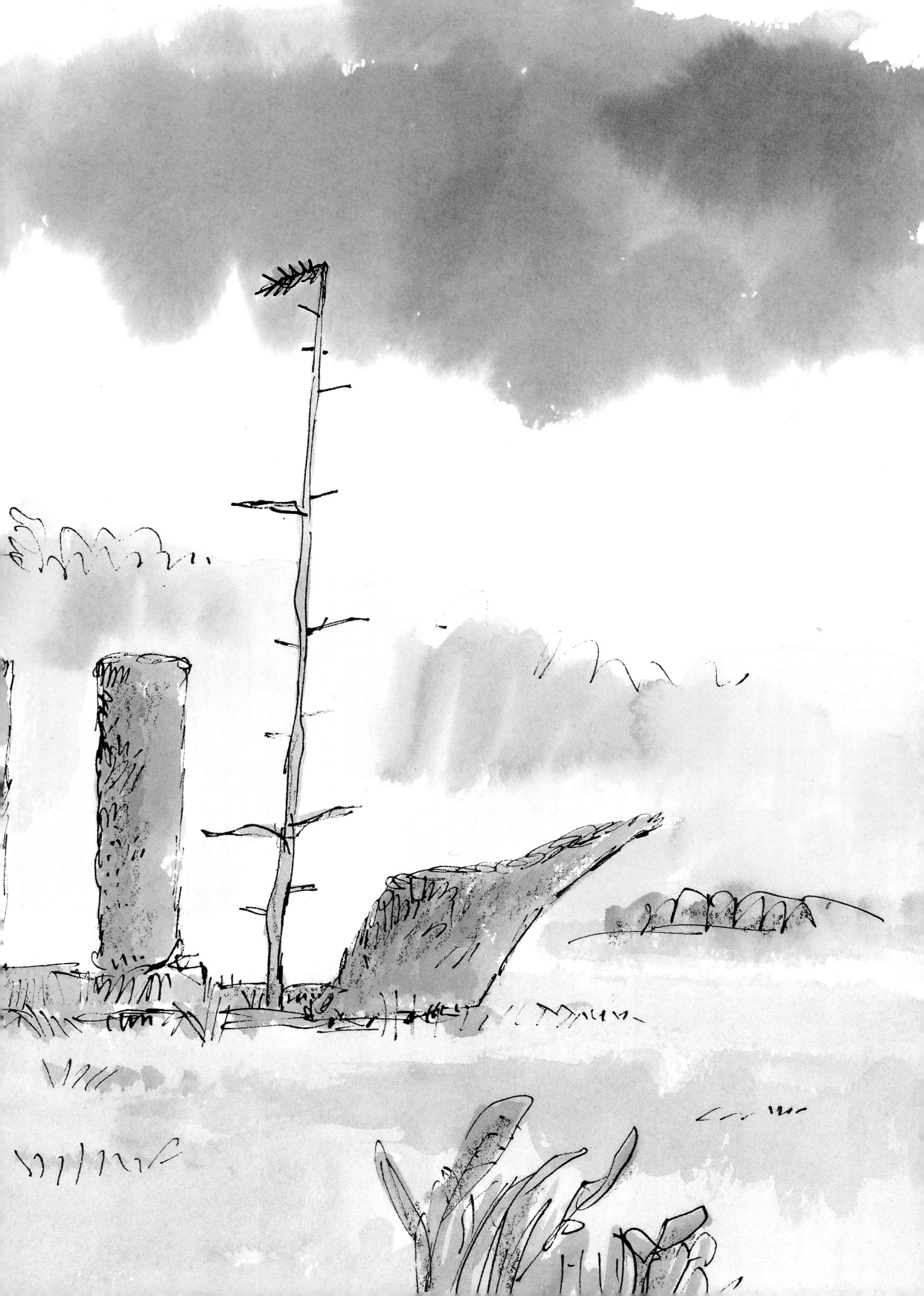

Towards the back of the ship there was also something like a tree house or a small garden shed perched on top of an ancient tree-stump. A set of wooden steps led up to it, and we climbed them and went in.

Inside there was a wheel with spokes that stuck out, just as if it were a proper ship. On a little shelf there was a telescope, and next to it a photo in a brown wooden frame of a man in uniform. From the roof hung an old lantern. Through the windows you could see for miles. You could almost believe you were at sea.

And then suddenly we were taken by surprise by a voice which said: "Well, what have we here, Bosun? Stowaways?"

There was a thin lady in a dark dress looking up at us.
"What do you think, Bosun? Shall we clap them in
irons?"

"Only youngsters," said the Bosun, who actually looked
more like a gardener. "Swabbin' the decks is the thing, if
you ask me."

"And after that perhaps we shall have tea on deck."

Swabbing the decks turned out to be sweeping away
the leaves; but tea really was tea, with madeira cake and
cucumber sandwiches. At the end of it Mrs Tredegar
(that was her name) said: "The Bosun will see you
ashore. And why not come aboard again tomorrow? I'm
sure that's what the Captain would have wished."

On our next visit Mrs Tredegar produced an old atlas, and every day after that we imagined that we were voyaging to some new place.

A flower urn became an Italian ruin;

a palm tree (there really was a palm tree) became the far-off shore of Egypt.

One chilly day we pretended we were in the Arctic. Bushes became icebergs and some sheep that had got into the garden by mistake became polar-bears.

The last few days of our holiday were hot and sunny.
They got hotter and hotter. We wore sunhats and
played deck-quoits and drank lots of limejuice. It
seemed as though we were heading southward through
tropical seas.

The next day was the last full day of our holiday and it
was agreed that we should stay overnight at the big
house. The weather was hotter than ever and
everything was absolutely still. And then, after tea, the
sky suddenly turned a strange colour and large drops
of rain began to fall. "There's going to be a storm,"
said Mrs Tredegar. "Come on, crew, into the
wheelhouse."

A huge warm wind blew through the garden.
Mrs Tredegar took the wheel.
"What would the captain have done?" she said.
"Steer into the eye of the storm. That's it.
Steer into the eye of the storm."

And what a storm it was!
There were huge claps of thunder; lightning
crackled across the whole of the sky.

The swaying of the lantern and the rain rushing
against the windows made it seem as though we were
truly at sea. And the storm seemed to go on for ever.

We still go back to see Mrs Tredegar every year. The Bosun says that he's getting too stiff to climb up and trim the masts and the funnels; and that Mrs Tredegar doesn't seem to mind.

And so gradually, year by year, the trees are growing back into their old shape; they are becoming ordinary trees, and soon there will no longer be any way at all of knowing that they were once the Green Ship.